THE 78-STORY TREEHOUSE

ANDY GRIFFITHS

illustrated by Terry Denton

SQUARE
FISH

Feiwel and Friends • New York

SQUARE FISH

An imprint of Macmillan Publishing Group, LLC
175 Fifth Avenue, New York, NY 10010
mackids.com

Library of Congress Control Number: 2017944808
ISBN 978-1-250-10483-0 (paperback) / ISBN 978-1-250-10484-7 (ebook)

Originally published as *The 78-Storey Treehouse* in Australia by Pan Macmillan
Australia Pty Ltd
Originally published in the United States by Feiwel and Friends
First Square Fish edition, 2019
Book designed by Rebecca Syracuse
Square Fish logo designed by Filomena Tuosto

10 9 8 7 6 5 4 3 2

AR: 3.6 / LEXILE: 560L

CONTENTS

CHAPTER 1

THE 78-STORY TREEHOUSE

Hi, my name is Andy.

This is my friend Terry.

We live in a tree.

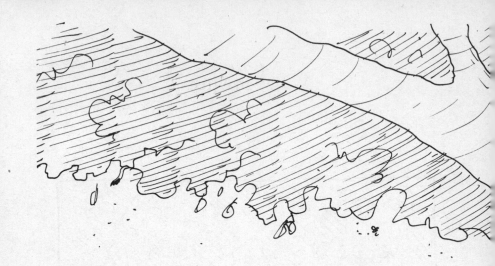

Well, when I say "tree," I mean treehouse. And when I say "treehouse," I don't just mean any old treehouse—I mean a 78-*story* treehouse!
(It used to be a 65-story treehouse, but we've added another 13 stories.)

So what are you waiting for?
Come on up!

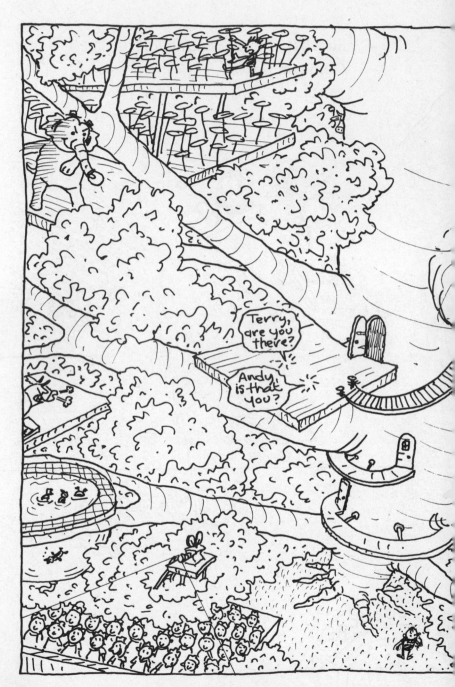

It's got a drive-through car wash (that you can drive through with the windows open and the roof down),

a combining machine,

a not-so-tight tightrope,

a 78-plate-spinning level,

a giant unhatched egg,

a courtroom with a robot judge called
Edward Gavelhead,

a scribbletorium,

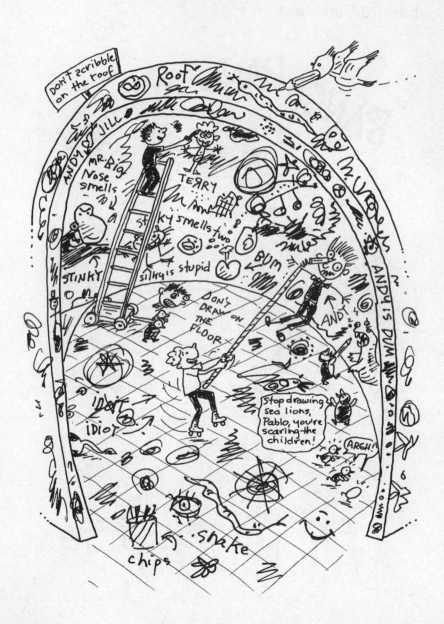

Andyland (a land full of Andy clones created in our cloning machine),

Terrytown (a crazy town full of Terry clones),

Jillville (a village full of Jills),

an ALL-BALL sports stadium (where you can play *every* ball sport in the whole world all at the same time),

an open-air movie theater with a super-giant screen,

and a high-security potato chip storage facility protected by 1,000 loaded mousetraps, 100 laser beams, a 10-ton weight, and one very angry duck.

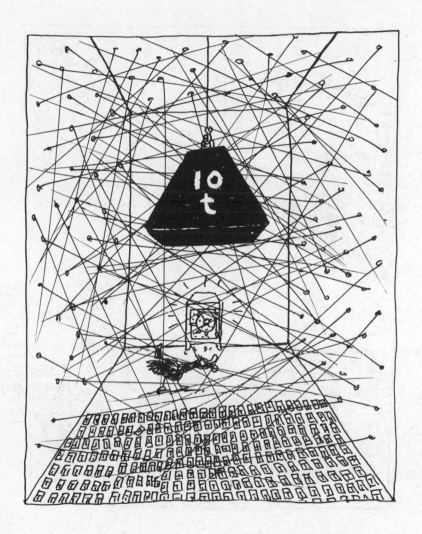

As well as being our home, the treehouse is also where we make books together. I write the words, and Terry draws the pictures.

As you can see, we've been doing this for quite a while now.

Sure, things can get crazy when you live in a
78-story treehouse . . .

But we always get our book written in the end . . .
somehow.

CHAPTER 2

TREEHOUSE: THE MOVIE

If you're like most of our readers, you're probably wondering if we're ever going to make a Treehouse movie. Well . . . guess what? We're making one right now!

We've got lights . . .

cameras . . .

chairs with our names
on the backs . . .

and a big-shot Hollywood movie director called Mr. Big Shot calling the shots. . . .

"CUT!" yells Mr. Big Shot. "That's BORING!"

"But that's how I *always* start the book," I say.

"This is NOT a book," barks Mr. Big Shot through his megaphone. "It's a MOVIE!"

"Well, yes," I say, "*I* know that and *you* know that, but I was just explaining it to the readers. . . ."

"Readers?" barks Mr. Big Shot. "I'm not interested in *readers*! I make MOVIES for movie fans who want ACTION, EXCITEMENT, and THRILLS, not *talking*! Who *are* you, anyway?"

"I'm *Andy*," I say. "I'm the narrator."

"Narrator?" says Mr. Big Shot. "We don't need a narrator."

"But I'm also one of the main characters."

"Hmmm," says Mr. Big Shot, frowning. "What about that other guy? The funny one with the curly hair. Where's he?"

"Here he comes now," I say as Terry runs onto the set with his pants on fire.

ARGHHHHHHHH!

Ants...

"Get out of the way!" says Terry, running between me and Mr. Big Shot. He reaches the edge of the deck and leaps off.

"Did he just jump into the shark tank?!" says Mr. Big Shot.

"Yep," I sigh. "That's Terry for you."

We peer over the edge.

"Are you all right?" shouts Mr. Big Shot.

"Much better now that my pants aren't on fire,"
says Terry.

"But you're in a tank full of man-eating sharks!"
says Mr. Big Shot.

"Yikes," says Terry. "I meant to jump into the
swimming pool!"

Terry swims to the side of the tank and tries to climb out. He's fast, but one of the sharks is faster. It surges up behind him,

opens its enormous mouth,

and chomps down on Terry's freshly barbecued
behind!

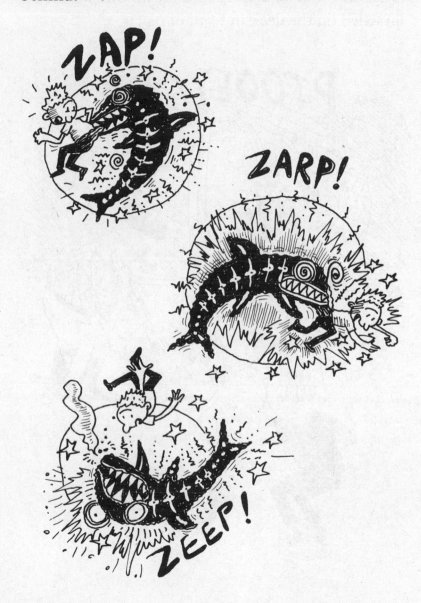

The electrocuted shark spits Terry out with such force that he flies up into the air and lands sprawled on the deck in front of us.

"That . . . was . . . *electrifying*!" says Mr. Big Shot.
"Here, let me help you up."

He reaches down and grabs Terry's hand.

The electric shock sends Mr. Big Shot flying backward. He crashes into one of the camera operators and then falls to the ground.

"Sorry," says Terry. "I must still be electricornified."

"Electri-*what*-ified?" says Mr. Big Shot.

"Well," says Terry, "I used the combining machine
to cross an electric eel

"with a unicorn

"to make an electricorn . . .

"but then a bolt of lightning shot out of the electricorn's horn,

"hit the back of my pants,

"and set them on fire."

Mr. Big Shot roars with laughter.

"What's so funny?" says Terry.

"You are," says Mr. Big Shot. "You're a LAUGH RIOT!!! This will make a great opening sequence for the movie!"

"But *I* always do the opening sequence!" I say.

"In the book, yes," says Mr. Big Shot. "But this is NOT a book . . . this is a movie! And Terry is going to be the star!"

"*Me?*" says Terry. "A movie star?"

"*Him?*" I say. "A movie star? But what about *me*?"

"I already told you," says Mr. Big Shot, "we don't need a narrator." He turns his attention back to Terry. "Is that electricorn still there?"

"Yes, I guess so," says Terry.

"Well, what are we waiting for?" says Mr. Big Shot. "Come on, everybody—except for Andy— let's go and film a reenactment!"

CHAPTER 3

SPIN, SPIN, SPIN

Fine.

So Mr. Big Shot doesn't want me in the movie.

I don't care.

It's not like I haven't got more important things
to do.

That giant unhatched egg, for instance—it's not
going to hatch itself.

I'd better go and sit on it right now!

I don't mind.

This is important work.

Much more important than making some
dumb movie.

Hang on.

That's a weird noise.

It sounds a bit like Jill and her intergalactic space-animal rescue service returning through the Earth's atmosphere.

WHOOSH!
PURRRR!
MIAOWW!

It *is* Jill and her intergalactic space-animal rescue service!

"Hi, Andy," says Jill. "I just got back from the moon. I had to rescue some mice whose rocket crashed while they were on a cheese-seeking mission. It doesn't seem to matter how many times I tell them the moon is *not* made of cheese, they just don't listen."

No cheese on moon!

Oh!

mouse space- ship

"Yeah, well, I'm doing some pretty important work here, too," I say. "I'm helping this giant unhatched egg hatch."

"That's great!" says Jill. "I can't wait to see what comes out."

"Me neither," I say.

"Where's Terry?" says Jill.

"He's with a film crew. They're making a Treehouse movie."

"Wow!" says Jill. "How come you're not there?"

I sigh. "The big-shot Hollywood director Mr. Big Shot said he didn't need a narrator."

"Isn't it called a 'voice-over' when it's in a movie?"

"Yeah, well, whatever it's called, Mr. Big Shot didn't want it."

"That's too bad," says Jill. "Still, a movie—that's pretty exciting!"

"I guess so," I say, "if you like electricorns, that is."

"*Electricorns?*" says Jill.

"Yeah," I say. "Terry used the combining machine to combine an electric eel and a unicorn. They're filming a reenactment."

"This I've *got* to see!" says Jill. "Good luck hatching the giant unhatched egg, Andy."

"Thanks, Jill," I say, but she doesn't hear me. She's already gone.

Never mind. I'll show them.

A giant unhatched egg is more exciting than a stupid old electricorn any day. . . . I mean, it could hatch any minute now . . . just you wait. . . .

Egg-hatching is great!

Egg-hatching is thrilling!

Egg-hatching is . . .

ZZZZZZZZZZZZZZZZZZZZZZZZZZZZZZZZZZZZZZZZZZZZZ
ZZZZZZZZZZZZZZZZZZZZZZZZZZZZZZZZZZZZZZZZZZZZZ
ZZZZZZZZZZZZZZZZZZZZZZZZZZZZZZZZZZZZZZZZZZZZZ
ZZZZZZZZZZZZZZZZZZZZZZZZZZZZZZZZZZZZZZZZZZZZZ
ZZZZZZZZZZZZZZZZZZZZZZZZZZZZZZZZZZZZZZZZZZZZZ
ZZZZZZZZZZZZZZZZZZZZZZZZZZZZZZZZZZZZZZZZZZZZZ
ZZZZZZZZZZZZZZZZZZZZZZZZZZZZZZZZZZZZZZZZZZZZZ
ZZZZZZZZZZZZZZZZZZZZZZZZZZZZZZZZZZZZZZZZZZZZZ
ZZZZZZZZZZZZZZZZZZZZZZZZZZZZZZZZZZZZZZZZZZZZZ
ZZZZZZZZZZZZZZZZZZZZZZZZZZZZZZZZZZZZZZZZZZZZZ
ZZZZZZZZZZZZZZZZZZZZZZZZZZZZZZZZZZZZZZZZZZZZZ
ZZZZZZZZZZZZZZZZZZZZZZZZZZZZZZZZZZZZZZZZZZZZZ
ZZZZZZZZZZZZZZZZZZZZZZZZZZZZZZZZZZZZZZZZZZZZZ
ZZZZZZZZZZZZZZZZZZZZZZZZZZZZZZZZZZZZZZZZZZZZZ
ZZZZZZZZZZZZZZZZZZZZZZZZZZZZZZZZZZZZZZZZZZZZZ
ZZZZZZZZZZZZZZZZZZZZZZZZZZZZZZZZZZZZZZZZZZZZZ

ZZZZZZZZZZZZZZZZZZZZZZZZZZZZZZZZZZZZZZZZZZZZZZZZZZZZZZ
ZZZZZZZZZZZZZZZZZZZZZZZZZZZZZZZZZZZZZZZZZZZZZZZZZZZZZZ
ZZZZZZZZZZZZZZZZZZZZZZZZZZZZZZZZZZZZZZZZZZZZZZZZZZZZZZ
ZZZZZZZZZZZZZZZZZZZZZZZZZZZZZZZZZZZZZZZZZZZZZZZZZZZZZZ
ZZZZZZZZZZZZZZZZZZZZZZZZZZZZZZZZZZZZZZZZZZZZZZZZZZZZZZ
ZZZZZZZZZZZZZZZZZZZZZZZZZZZZZZZZZZZZZZZZZZZZZZZZZZZZZZ
ZZZZZZZZZZZZZZZZZZZZZZZZZZZZZZZZZZZZZZZZZZZZZZZZZZZZZZ
ZZZZZZZZZZZZZZZZZZZZZZZZZZZZZZZZZZZZZZZZZZZZZZZZZZZZZZ

Oh . . . I must have dozed off . . . That's the videophone. I'd better answer it. It's probably Mr. Big Nose.

"Hi, Mr. Big Nose," I say. "I guess you're calling about the book."

"Book?" says Mr. Big Nose. "No, I'm calling to find out how the movie is going."

"Well," I say, "I don't know if the movie is going to work out quite the way I'd hoped. . . ."

"Are you kidding?" says Mr. Big Nose. "I've spent a fortune on Big Nose Books product placement. So you'd better *make* it work!"

"I'm not sure I'm comfortable with all this advertising," I say, but Mr. Big Nose has already hung up.

"Why are you still here?" says Mr. Big Shot, climbing up onto my level. "Haven't you got a home to go to?"

"The treehouse *is* my home," I say. "I live here."

"Well, just keep out of the way," says Mr. Big Shot. "We're about to film the scene where Terry painted a cat yellow and turned it into a catnary."

"But I was there!" I say. "I was in that story. I tried to stop him!"

"Well, we can't have that, can we?" says Mr. Big Shot. "I think moviegoers will *love* to see a flying cat, so if you could just keep off the set, that would be great."

"But . . . ," I say. "Terry! Tell him!"

Terry shrugs. "Sorry, Andy, but it's not really my decision. Mr. Big Shot *is* the director. . . ."

They all head off up to the observation deck.

Fine.

Film the scene without me.

See if I care.

I've not only got to help this giant unhatched egg hatch, but I've also got 78 plates to spin!

Plates don't just keep spinning all by themselves, you know.

And plate-spinning is a *lot* of fun. Even *more* fun than giant unhatched egg-hatching.

Looks like I've arrived just in time—some of those plates are really wobbly. They're about to fall off their poles!

Well, I'll soon fix that . . .

spin . . . spin . . . spin . . . spin . . . spin . . . spin . . .
spin . . . spin . . . spin . . . spin . . . spin . . . spin . . .
spin . . . spin . . . spin . . . spin . . . spin . . . spin . . .
spin . . . spin . . .

spin ... spin ... spin ... spin ... spin ... spin ...
spin ... spin ... spin ... spin ... spin ... spin ...
spin ... spin ... spin ... spin ... spin ... spin ...
spin ... spin ... spin ... spin ... spin ... spin ...
spin ...

See what I mean?

Plate-spinning is better than making a dumb old movie any day.

Uh-oh . . .

I think I might have spun them a bit too hard. . . .

WHIZZZZZZZzzzz!

WHIZZZZZZzzzz!

WHIZZZZZZZZZzzz!

WHIZZZZZZZZZ!

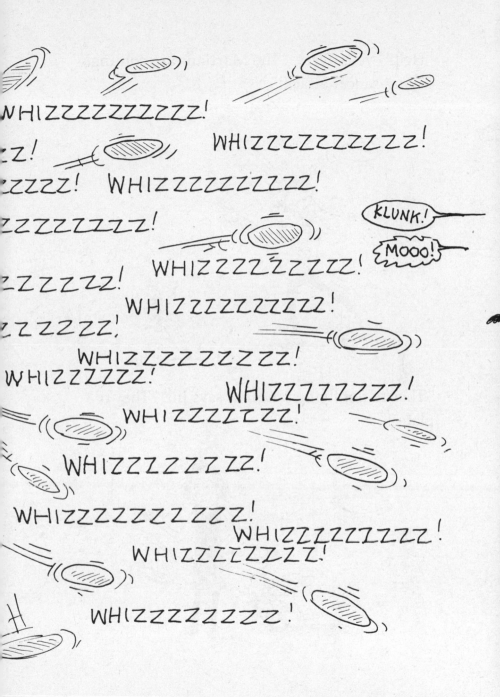

"Help!" yells Terry. "The Martians are coming! Flying-saucer attack!"

"They're not flying saucers," says Jill. "They're plates!"

"CUT!" yells Mr. Big Shot. "NO PLATE-THROWING ON SET!"

"Sorry," I say.

"You should be more careful," says Jill. "One of those plates almost hit Silky!"

"It was an accident!" I say. "I just spun them a little bit too hard and they spun off their spinners!"

"Well, lucky for you we just finished that scene anyway," says Mr. Big Shot. "Now we're going to film a reenactment of the time the sharks ate Terry's underpants."

shark
dream
↓

"But it's cruel to do that to the sharks again," I say. "They got really sick!"

"It's okay, Andy," says Jill. "It's just *pretend*. They're not *real* underpants. They're prop underpants, with fish paste. It's actually a treat for the sharks—and they're really excited about being in the movie."

Mixer

Shark whisperer

"So if you could just run along now, Andy," says Mr. Big Shot, patting me on the head. "There's a good narrator."

"But you can't make the whole movie without me!" I say. "I was there. I was part of the story!"

"We're not making it without you," says Mr. Big Shot. "We've got Mel Gibbon to play you."

"Mel Gibson?" I say. "He's a bit old, isn't he?"

"Not Mel Gibson," says Mr. Big Shot. "Mel *Gibbon*. Look, here he comes now!"

"But he's a monkey!" I say.

"No, he's not," says Mr. Big Shot, "he's a gibbon. And he's also one of the hottest young primates working in film today. Plus, he works for peanuts—literally!"

"But *I'll* work for free!" I say. "And I'll make a more convincing Andy than some monkey. Watch this!"

"Hi, my name is Andy
   . . . this is my friend Terry
   . . . we live in a tree
   . . . well, when I say 'tree'—"

"How many times do I have to tell you?" says Mr. Big Shot. "WE DON'T NEED A NARRATOR!"

"I'm not narrating," I say, "I'm *acting* like a narrator!"

"Sounds a lot like narrating to me," says Mr. Big Shot.

"And to me," says Terry.

"You're a *good* Andy, Andy," says Jill. "But I think Mel is better. He's more *convincing*."

"Yeah, and he's also funnier," says Terry.

"But you hate monkeys," I say.

"I know I do," says Terry. "But Mel's not a monkey—he's a gibbon."

"This is ridiculous," I say, shaking my head. "I don't believe it."

Mel comes over to me.

"Look," he says in a low voice, "I understand you're upset. If it's any comfort, I don't like it any more than you do. I was hoping to play Terry. But let's try to be professional about it, okay?"

"Professional?" I say. "The only thing professional about *you* is that you're a professional *thief*. You just stole my part in the movie."

"I didn't *steal* your part, I was *cast*," says Mel.

"Whatever!" I say, stomping off the set. "If anybody wants the *real* me, I'll be in the scribbletorium."

But nobody takes any notice, of course. They're all too busy making their dumb old movie.

CHAPTER 4

SCRIBBLE, SCRIBBLE, SCRIBBLE

I don't know about you, but I find that scribbling really helps take my mind off things. It's much more fun than making a movie.

And the best thing about scribbling is that it's *so* simple! All you need is something to scribble with . . .

and a scribbletorium . . .

and then you just scribble!

And scribble . . .

and scribble . . .

and scribble . . .

and scribble . . .

and scribble.

See-through glass wall ↗

And scribble! And scribble! And scribble!

And scribble! And scribble! And scribble!

And scribble! And scribble! And scribble!

86

And scribble! And scribble! And scribble!

And scribble! And scribble! And scribble!

And scribble! And scribble! And scribble!

Uh-oh. . . .

You know what I said about how scribbling is really simple?

Well, I forgot to say that it can also be quite messy.

Especially if you scribble so much that the scribbletorium explodes and scribble goes all over the treehouse.

"CUT! CUT! CUT!" yells Mr. Big Shot.
"WHO SCRIBBLED ALL OVER THE SET?"

"Not me," says Terry.
"Not me," says Mel.
"Not me," says Jill.

"I'm sorry, everybody," I say. "It was an accident."

Mel snorts. "Sure it was," he says. "You did it on purpose."

"Go eat a banana, Monkey-boy!" I shout at him.

Mel bursts into tears, and Terry and Jill rush to his side to comfort him.

"Andy!" says Jill. "You really need to calm down. I know you're upset, but being mean to a monkey— I mean, gibbon—well, that's *inexcusable*."

"I'm sorry I was mean to the monkey," I say, "but I didn't mean for the scribble to go everywhere. I just got carried away."

"I wish I could believe you, Andy," says Jill, "but I think you're being a bad sport . . . and, worse, a bad *friend*. This is Terry's big break—can't you be happy for him?"

"I *am* happy for him," I say, "and I'm *trying* to be a good friend, but he's not being a good friend to me. He's too busy being a big-shot movie star. And then he'll probably just go off to Hollywood and leave me here all alone."

"I don't think Terry would do that," says Jill.
"Do what?" says Terry.
"Go off to Hollywood and leave Andy here all by himself."

"Of course not!" says Terry. "You could come with me, Andy. I'll need somebody to carry my bags. You can be my butler!"

"BUTLER?!" I say.

"Quiet on the set!" says Mr. Big Shot.

"BUTLER?!" I say again, only louder

this time. I can't believe he just suggested I could be his butler.

"I said 'quiet,' and I mean it!" shouts Mr. Big Shot.

"BUTLER?" I say again, even louder than before.

"I DON'T WANNA BE YOUR DUMB BUTLER!"

"Right! That does it!" says Mr. Big Shot. "I've had enough of your plate-throwing, scribbling, and shouting. You are banned from the set!"

"The treehouse is not a 'set'!" I say. "It's my *home.*
And not even a big bossy boots like you can ban
me from my *own home.*"

"Oh yes, I can," says Mr. Big Shot. "Watch this!"
He picks me up and boots me out of the tree.

CHAPTER 5

DAY OF THE LIVING PUDDLE

So here I am.

Kicked out of my own home.

Sitting in a puddle.

Yes, that's right. I landed in a puddle.

And to make things worse, the puddle is getting bigger.

And bigger.

And bigger.

And bigger!

Uh-oh—this is no ordinary puddle. This is the sort of puddle that will just keep getting bigger and bigger and bigger and bigger until it empuddles the whole world. . . .

ABOVE: *An artist's impression of a puddle empuddling planet Earth.*

But never fear . . . as well as making books, Terry and I are the greatest puddle-fighting duo the world has ever known.

We are every puddle's worst nightmare. Terry stomps them and then I suck them up with a straw. *The Stomper* and *The Sucker* ... (Come to think of it, our story would make a great movie!)

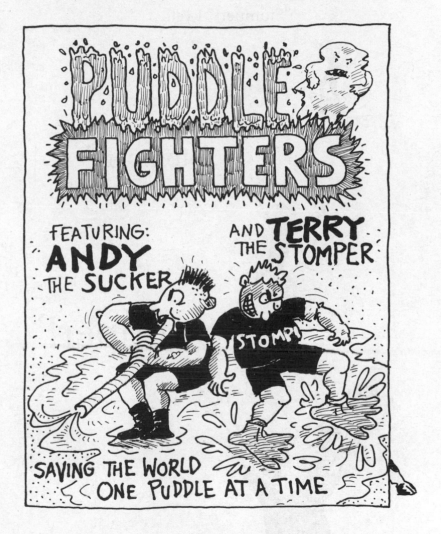

But this is no time to be thinking about movies. This is real life. I have to send out the secret puddle-fighting call and get the old team back together!

"Stomper!" I yell.

"Stomper!"

"Stomper!"

"It's no use," says the puddle. "Nothing can stop me from empuddling your treehouse!"

"Oh, yeah?" I say, removing my T-shirt to reveal my secret puddle-fighting identity. "You just picked a fight with the wrong guy. I'm *The Sucker!*"

"You're a sucker all right," sneers the puddle. "A sucker for punishment!"

"No," I say, "not *that* sort of sucker."

I pull a supersize drinking straw from the quiver on my back and wave it menacingly at the puddle.

"You'll never drink me alive!" says the puddle.

"That's what you think!" I say.

I put the straw up to my mouth and bend down.

"Oh, no you don't," says the puddle.

It rises up like an enormous wave and crashes down on top of me.

Over and over I tumble. Only my straw keeps me afloat. . . .

The puddle gets me in a headlock,

but then I get the puddle in a headlock.

"I've got you now!" I say. I stick the straw into the
puddle and start sucking . . .

and sucking . . .

and sucking . . .

and sucking . . .

and sucking . . .

and sucking . . .

and sucking . . .

and sucking.

And the puddle starts to shrink . . .

and shrink . . .

and shrink . . .

and shrink.

And I keep sucking . . .

and sucking . . .

and sucking . . .

and sucking . . .

until, at last, the puddle is nothing but sludgy brown sludge.

If only Mr. Big Shot had been filming that! It would make a much better movie than all of Terry's fake reenactments put together.

Hang on.

Maybe he *was* filming it!

Maybe Mr. Big Shot arranged for this whole thing to happen so he could secretly record it.

I look around but I can't see anything except a few dumb-looking cows.

Never mind.

I can't really think about all that right now because I've got a more urgent problem.

Will you excuse me for a moment, readers?

I may be some time, so do feel free to go on to the next chapter, and I'll join you there.

CHAPTER 6

TROUBLE IN ANDYLAND

Ah, that's better.

Thanks for waiting.

Now, where was I?

Let me see. . . . Ah yes, I remember now.

Mr. Big Shot kicked me out of the treehouse . . .
and I landed in a puddle . . . and we had a big fight
. . . and I sucked it up . . . and then I had to go to
the bathroom.

But what now?

Where can I go?

I can't hang out with Terry because he's too
busy being a big-shot Hollywood movie star.

And I can't hang out with Jill because she's too busy helping to wrangle the animals for the movie.

Hang on, I know who I can hang out with . . . a bunch of the funniest, smartest, and best-looking guys in the world. Yep, you guessed it—I'm off to . . .

ANDYLAND! I'll have lots of friends here because everybody is me! As the sign says, it's THE ANDY-EST PLACE ON EARTH.

"Hi, Andy!" I say to the Andy guarding the gate.

"Who goes there?" he says.

"It's *me*," I say.

"Who?"

"*Andy!*"

"I'm afraid I'm going to need to see some identification," he says.

"But you only have to *look* at me!" I say. "I look exactly like you."

He shrugs. "I know," he says, "but we're being extra careful. We had some cows try to sneak in disguised as Andys the other day."

"*Cows?*" I say.

"Yeah," says the guard, shaking his head. "Go figure. But don't worry, we caught them, milked them, and sent them on their way."

"Wow, I had no idea cows could be so sneaky," I say.

"Yep," says the guard, "which is why I'm going to need proof that you're a true Andy and not an impostor."

"What sort of proof?"

"Hmmm . . . let me see," he says, stroking his chin. "What's two plus two?"

Uh-oh. I can't even count from one to ten in the right order. I've got no hope of solving a sum as difficult as this!

"Er, ah, um . . ." I stutter. "Um, er, errr, errrrr, um, ummm, ah, umm, errr, um, ah, er, eep, ah . . . I don't know."

"I don't know, either," the Andy guard says. "Congratulations, Andy, you passed the test! You may enter."

"Thanks, Andy!" I say, stepping through the gate.

"Hi, Andy!" yell a bunch of Andys coming
toward me.

"Hi, Andys!" I yell back. "What's up?"

"*You* are!" say the Andys, lifting me onto their
shoulders and carrying me down the main street.

I *love* coming to Andyland.

More and more cheering Andys come out onto the street until there are so many Andys, we can't go any farther.

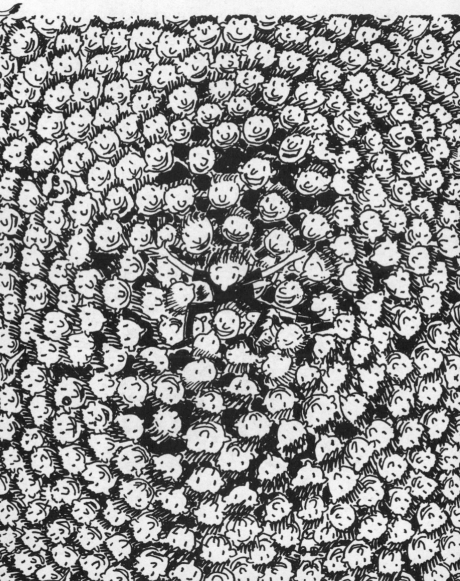

They are chanting my name.

"AN-DY! AN-DY! AN-DY!"

(Or are they just chanting their *own* names?
It's a bit hard to tell with Andys. They're kind of
excitable.)

The chanting is getting louder and louder. It's time
for me to speak to them.

The Andys lower me to the ground. Then they arrange themselves in a pyramid and help me climb up.

A cheer goes up from the crowd.

"Quiet down, everyandy," I say.

But they don't quiet down. They're getting louder. And louder. And louder.

"Everyandy!" I yell. "SHUT UP!"

"No!" they yell. "YOU shut up!"

"No," I say. "YOU shut up!"

"No, YOU shut up!" they say.

"No, YOU shut up!" I yell.

"No, YOU shut up!" they yell back.

"No," I shout as loudly as I can. "YOU shut up infinity times more than whatever *you* say!"

The Andys are silent. You've got to hand it to me: I sure know how to shut my selves up.

"Thank you!" I say. "And thanks for the parade.
I love parades."

"WE KNOW!" they yell in unison.

"It is good to know that I can count on Andys like
you to cheer me up."

"WE KNOW!" they yell again.

"You will be pleased to hear that I will be
staying in Andyland until they finish filming the
Treehouse movie."

The Andys gasp. "There's going to be a movie?" they say.

"Yes," I say, "but—"

"YAY!" shouts the crowd. "A Treehouse movie! We're going to be movie stars! We're going to be famous!"

"Hold on," I shout. "Before you get too excited, you should know one thing: *we are not in it.* We've been replaced by a monkey, and Terry is the star."

The Andys gasp again. "TERRY is the star?"

"Yeah," I say, shrugging. "I'm as surprised as you are. He's not even that funny."

"Yes, he is!" say the Andys. "Terry is *really* funny!
We *love* Terry!"

"No, we don't," I say.

"YES, WE DO!" shout the Andys. "TERRY is
COOL!"

"No," I say, "he's NOT!"

"Yes, he *is*," say the Andys. "Infinity times more than whatever *you* say!"

Darn. They've got me there, but, hey, who can blame them? They learned from the master.

"Okay, you win," I say. "But it doesn't change the fact that we're not in the movie."

"Who cares?!" they shout. "Terry is our favorite anyway. Let's go see the filming!"

"Bad idea," I say. "We've been banned from the set."

But the Andys just ignore me. They're too busy charging up Andy Street toward the main gate.

"No," I yell. "Wait! Come back! You're supposed to be on my side!"

"We are," they say, surging past me. "But we like Terry better. Sorry!"

The Andys swarm out of Andyland . . .

up the ladder . . .

and onto the observation deck, where Mr. Big Shot
is filming a reenactment of the time Terry got
caught in a burp-gas-filled bubble-gum bubble.

"Hey!" yells Mr. Big Shot. "No Andys on the set!"

But the Andys ignore Mr. Big Shot. They just keep climbing . . . and climbing . . . and climbing . . .

Mel Gibbon is whacking golf balls at the Andys,
trying to hold them back, but there are too many
Andys . . . and not enough golf balls.

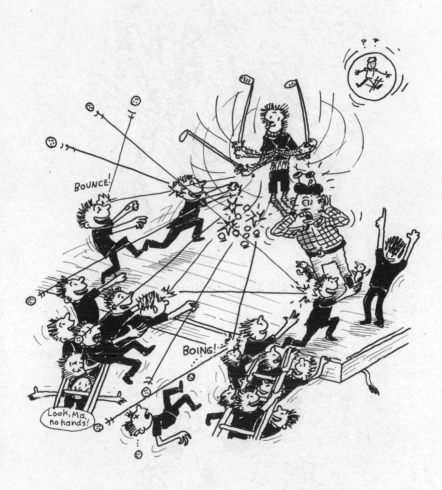

The observation deck—overloaded with way too many Andys—is swaying dangerously.

"Abandon set!" yells Mr. Big Shot. "ABANDON SET!"

But it's too late. There is an enormous *crack* . . . the
observation deck crumbles, and we all crash into
the forest below.

CHAPTER 7

COWDUGGERY!

All the Andys land in a big sprawling pile . . .

but I land headfirst in a nearby prickle bush. The Andys are groaning and yelling and shouting as they try to untangle themselves. Some of them are angry.

Some are laughing. And some are crying. Which is understandable. They've—I mean, *we've*—all had a pretty big fall.

Mr. Big Shot crawls out from under the pile of Andys and stands in front of them, his hands on his hips. "Which one of you clowns is the *real* Andy?" he demands.

"Me!" they all shout. "Me!" "Me!" "Me!" "Me!"
"Me!" "Me!" "Me!" "Me!" "Me!" "Me!" "Me!" "Me!"
"Me!" "Me!" "Me!" "Me!" "Me!" "Me!" "Me!" "Me!"
"Me!" "Me!" "Me!" "Me!" "Me!" "Me!" "Me!" "Me!"
"Me!" "Me!" "Me!" "Me!" "Me!" "Me!" "Me!"

"Let me put it another way then," growls Mr. Big Shot, rolling up his sleeves. "Nobody destroys my set and gets away with it. So which one of you wants to die first?"

"Not me!" shout the Andys. "Not me!"

I know at this point I should come out of hiding
and rescue the Andys, but, hey, I don't want to die
any more than they do. And it's their own fault,
after all. I mean, I *did* try to stop them.

"I don't think any of them are the *real* Andy," says Jill, studying the Andy clones carefully. "I know him pretty well, and none of these Andys look *quite* right."

"Then where is he?" says Mr. Big Shot.

"Probably hiding," says Mel Gibbon. "He obviously put the Andys up to this to disrupt the filming. Pretty low trick to get a bunch of clueless clones to do your dirty work for you—but that's obviously the sort of person he is."

"Well, he'll find out what sort of person *I* am if he ever dares to show his face around here again," says Mr. Big Shot, pulling his cameras and camera operators from the pile. "Come on, you lot," he barks. "We've got to rebuild that observation deck and get this movie back on track. Let's go!"

As Mr. Big Shot and the crew leave, one of
the Andys turns to Terry and says, "Sorry we
disrupted your movie, but it's not really our fault—
you are a terrible observation-deck builder."

"It's not *my* fault!" says Terry. "The deck wasn't designed to hold so many Andys. It's *Andy's* fault for letting you all out of Andyland."

I want to yell, "I DIDN'T LET THEM OUT! I TRIED TO STOP THEM, BUT THEY WOULDN'T LISTEN!" but that would mean giving away my hiding place and, all things considered, it's probably best for *this* Andy to stay hidden for the time being.

"Come on, Andys," says one of the Andys. "Let's go back to Andyland. It's more fun there. And, Terry, if you see Andy, can you tell him we'd prefer he doesn't visit for a while? I think we need a little break from each other."

"Sure," says Terry. "I know *exactly* how you feel."

And with that, the Andys start hobbling and limping their way back to Andyland.

"Poor Andy," says Jill. "He must be really upset to have done something like this. Maybe you should go and find him, Terry, and tell him you're not mad at him."

"But I *am* mad at him," says Terry. "Just because he's not in the movie he wants to wreck it for everybody else."

"I know it *looks* like that," says Jill as she and Terry and Mel start walking back toward the treehouse, "but maybe there's another side to the story. I'm not sure we can believe everything those Andys are telling us."

"Or anything the *real* Andy tells us, either," says Mel.

I'm climbing out of the prickle bush when I hear voices. And mooing. And the unmistakable sound of cud-chewing.

A pair of trench-coated figures emerge from the trees on the other side of the clearing. They are holding microphones and recording equipment. Which is kind of weird . . . given that they are cows.

I'm going to sneak up on them and find out what they're up to. I'm pretty well camouflaged with these prickles all over me—I just need something to cover my head.

I look around. All I can see is a whole bunch of dried-up old cowpats. Disgusting . . . but perfect! I pick one up, put it on my head, and begin commando-crawling toward the cows.

As I get closer, I hear one of them moo: "Those crazy humans don't suspect a thing."

"Yeah," moos the other one. "They have no idea that we have secretly infiltrated their treehouse with many spy cows such as ourselves and that we are stealing their movie, scene by scene, to make our own *mooo*-vie. For years the humans have milked us. Now we're milking them . . . for their ideas! Let's see how *they* like it!"

One of the spy cows moos quietly into a hoof-held walkie-talkie. "Attention, all movie-idea-stealing spy cows! The film crew, director, and actors are heading back into the treehouse. Stay alert . . . *and* out of sight!"

So that's what they're up to! If there's one thing in the world I hate more than movie-idea stealing, it's movie-idea-stealing spy cows!

I've got to go and warn Mr. Big Shot right away! Then he—and everybody else—will see that I'm *not* trying to wreck the movie. Mr. Big Shot will probably be so impressed he'll rehire me and give me a starring role.

There's no time to lose! I creep across the path to our front door and—when the spy cows aren't watching—slip inside.

I climb the stairs and poke my head up into the first story.

"Eek!" says Jill. "A peeping cowpat!"

"Urgh!" says Terry. "Cowpats are disgusting!"

"GET THAT COWPAT OFF MY SET!" barks
Mr. Big Shot.

"I'm not a cowpat!" I say. "It's me, Andy! I'm just
wearing a cowpat hat for camouflage! I came
to warn you that there are a bunch of spy cows
spying on you. They're going to steal all your ideas
and make their own mooo-vie."

"Do you really expect us to believe such a preposterous story?" says Mr. Big Shot.

"I know it sounds crazy," I say, "but it's true! I saw them! And I heard them!"

"I really don't think cows would do that," says Jill. "They are such honest, trustworthy animals."

"Not these ones," I say. "They're *spy* cows! And if you don't believe me, go back through the book and see for yourself. There's a spy cow hiding on *every single page!*"*

It's true . . . there really is. And sometimes there's even more than one.

"Are you out of your mind?!" says Mr. Big Shot.
"We've got a movie to make. We haven't got time
to be looking at boring old books—especially ones
that haven't even been written yet."

"Fine!" I say. "I was only trying to help. Let the spy
cows steal your stupid movie. See if *I* care!"

"Hey, Andy," says Mel Gibbon. "If what you say is true, why don't you go and audition for the mooo-vie-making cows? You make a very convincing cowpat!"

"Yeah," says Terry, "you not only look the part, but you smell like one, too!"

"High-five, my hu-man!" says Mel, holding up his paw.

Terry high-fives him, and they both dissolve into helpless giggling.

"Guess I'll be going, then," I say. "Have fun with your new best friend, Terry. Good-bye . . . FOREVER!"

CHAPTER 8

MY AUTOBIOGRAPHY OF MY LIFE BY ME (AND NOT TERRY)

I stomp down the stairs, go out the front door, and fling my cowpat hat into the forest. The movie is not my problem anymore. And neither is Terry. We are done.

Who needs him anyway? Not me. I can draw my own pictures. And now I can finally get started on the autobiography I've always wanted to write.

I feel a hand on my shoulder and look up. It's Jill.

"I came to see if you were okay," she says.

"Yeah, I'm fine," I say. "I'm quite busy, actually. I'm writing my autobiography."

"That's great, Andy," says Jill, "but won't Terry be too busy to illustrate it?"

"Yeah, probably," I say, "but it doesn't matter because I can do it myself. Look."

I hand Jill the pages.

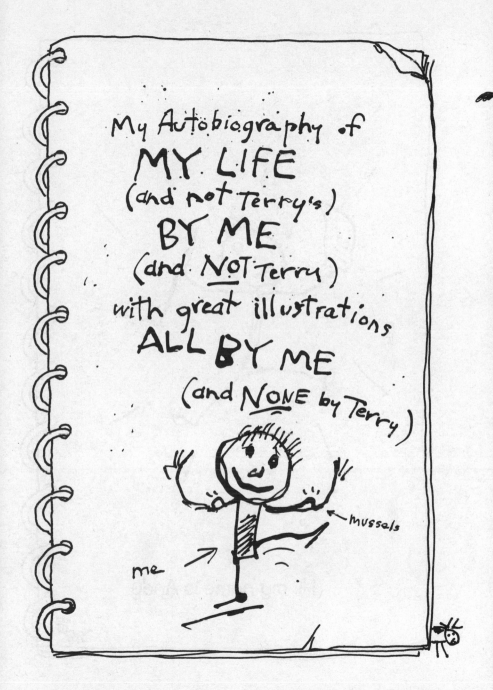

My Autobiography of
MY LIFE
(and not Terry's)
BY ME
(and NOT Terry)
with great illustrations
ALL BY ME
(and NONE by Terry)

me →

← mussels

Hi, my name is Andy.

I used to have a friend called Terry, but he's not my friend anymore because he's a stupid dumb dum-dum,

and his new best friend is a monkey
called Mel Gibbon who stole my
part in the movie,

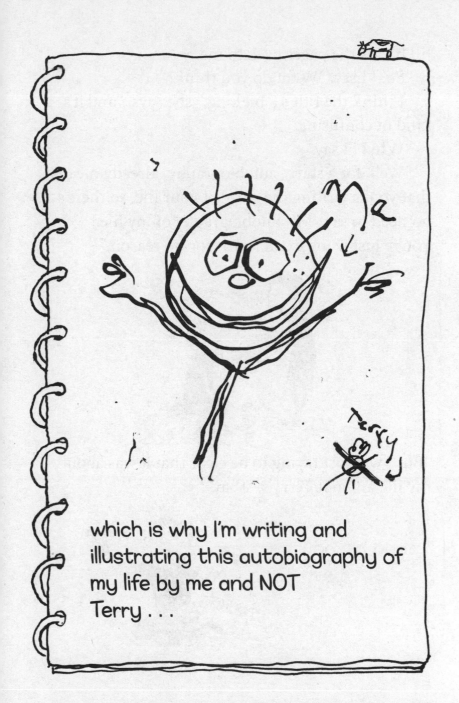

which is why I'm writing and
illustrating this autobiography of
my life by me and NOT
Terry . . .

Jill hands the pages back to me.

"So?" I say. "What do you think?"

"I think the title's a bit long," she says, "and it's kind of confusing."

"Why?" I say.

"Well, for a start, 'autobiography' already means that you're writing the story of your life, so there's no need to say, 'My autobiography of my life.' You're just using extra words for no reason."

"But I was just trying to be clear that it was about my life and not Terry's," I say.

"Well, that's another thing," says Jill. "You say it's about you, but all you're really doing is going on and on about Terry and, I don't mean to be rude, but it isn't very nice . . . and it's a little bit boring."

"Yeah, I guess you're right," I say. "Terry isn't very nice and he can be quite boring. I'll make a new one."

I write another version as fast as I can and give it to Jill.

"Is this better?" I say.

MY
AUTOBIOGRAPHY
BY ME
(ANDY)

My autobiography begins on a dark
and stormy night in a spooky old
castle owned by the evil genius
Doctor Von Fearstein.

I was awoken by the sound of mysterious noises coming from Doctor Von Fearstein's underground laboratory.

Even though Doctor Von Fearstein had forbidden me ever to enter his laboratory, I decided to investigate.

With only a feeble candle to light my path, I made my way down the creaky, crumbling staircase . . .

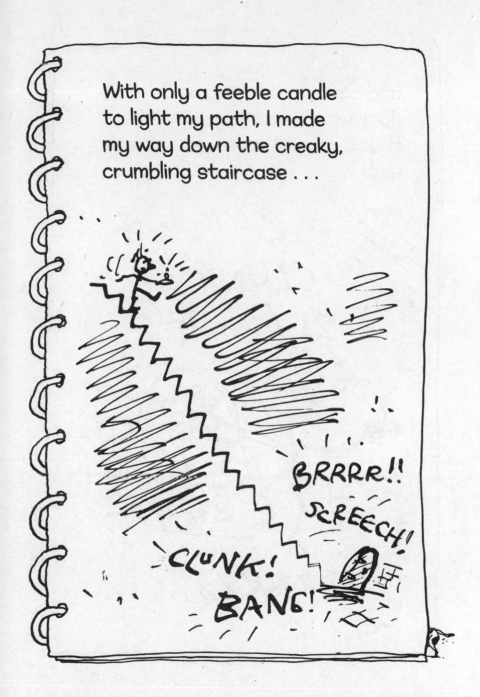

and came to a heavy wooden door with a warning sign on it that said, WARNING! DO NOT ENTER OR ELSE.

So, of course, I had no choice—
I had to enter. I pushed the door
open . . . and came face-to-face
with Doctor Von Fearstein's
most terrifying creation . . .

"Stop it, Andy!" says Jill. "It's too scary!"

"Yeah, I know," I say. "But it's pretty exciting, isn't it?"

"I suppose so," she says, "but . . . an autobiography is supposed to be true, not a made-up horror story. You're supposed to tell the *true* story of *your* life."

"Hmmm," I say. "These autobiographies are trickier than I thought. There are a lot of rules."

"Just imagine you're telling a reader the true story of your life from the very beginning," says Jill. "That's not so hard, is it?"

"No," I say, picking up my pen again.

I write a new version and hand it to her.

THE TRUE AUTOBIOGRAPHY OF MY LIFE FROM THE VERY BEGINNING BY ME

If you're like most of my readers, you're probably wondering how I got to be so AWESOME! Well, it's a fascinating story . . .

It all started when I was born.

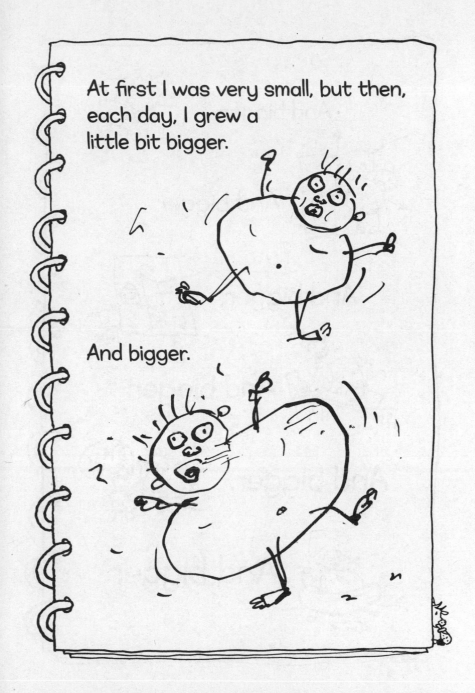

At first I was very small, but then, each day, I grew a little bit bigger.

And bigger.

And bigger.

And bigger.

And bigger.

And bigger.

And bigger.

And bigger.

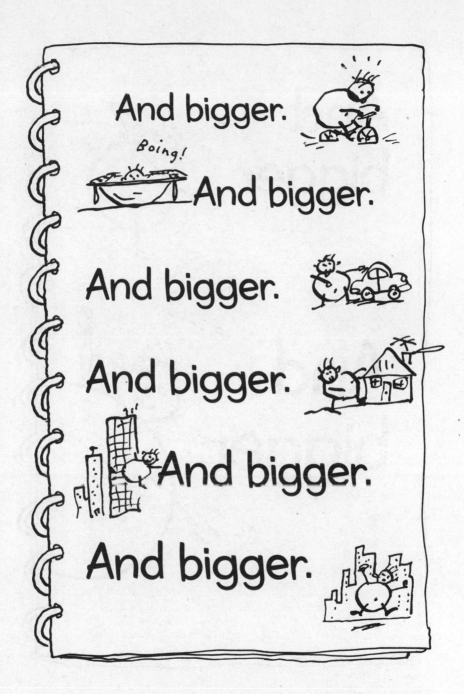

And bigger.

Boing!

And bigger.

And bigger.

And bigger.

And bigger.

And bigger.

And
bigger.

And
bigger.

And
bigger.

And

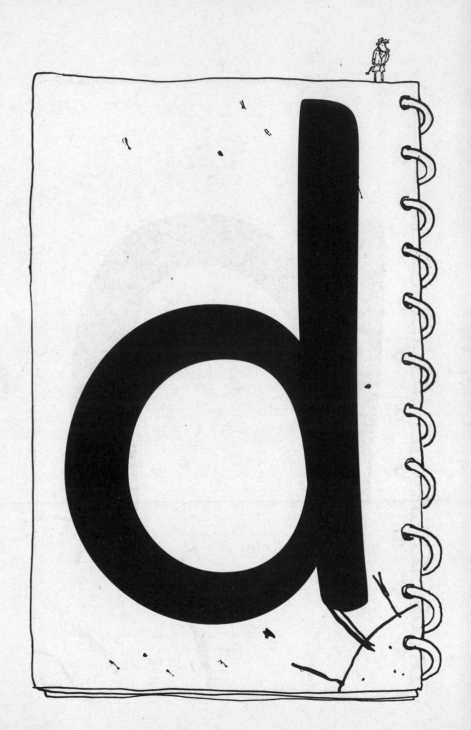

"ANDY!" shouts Jill. "Stop writing, 'And bigger. And bigger. And bigger!'"

"But why?" I say. "It's *true!*"

"It may be true," says Jill, "but it's not very interesting."

"But I *tried* to make it interesting and you said it had to be true."

"You need to make it true *and* interesting," says Jill.

"I give up!" I say. "Writing an autobiography is just *too* hard."

Suddenly animal noises start coming out of Jill's pocket.

"Excuse me, Andy," says Jill, checking the screen of her intergalactic space-animal rescue service emergency pager.

"Uh-oh," she says. "There's an intergalactic space-animal emergency on Planet Zonkatroid. A space-ladybug's house is on fire and she's not home. I have to go and put it out immediately. Here comes my team now!"

Jill jumps aboard her space-cat-powered
intergalactic space-animal rescue spacecraft.

"I'll see you, later, Andy," she says.

"Yeah, see you, Jill," I say, but she doesn't hear me.
She's already gone.

I'm all alone. Again.

Some day this is turning out to be. I've been fired
from my own movie and replaced by a monkey.
Abandoned by my own best friend. Kicked out of
my own treehouse. Disowned by my own clones
and banned from Andyland, my own kingdom.

And as if all that isn't bad enough, now I've failed at writing my own autobiography. Fail. Fail. Fail. Fail. Fail.

I guess there's only one thing left to do. Yep, you guessed it. I need to remember my favorite inspiring motivational quote that always helps me when I'm feeling down and think I can't go on. Now, let me see, what is it? I think it's something about chips. . . .

When the chips are down ...

Um ...

Er ...

Ah ...

Hmm ...

I'm having *such* a bad day I can't even remember my favorite inspiring motivational quote.

Is it *When the chips are down, and you feel like you can't go on, that's when you know you're halfway there?*

No, that's not it. Not even close.

Maybe it's *When the chips are down, the chips get going.*

That's more like it, but no, it's still not quite right. . . .

Hang on! I remember now!

When the chips are down, go eat some chips.

YES! That's it!

The chips *are* down so that's exactly what I'm going to do!

I'm going to go to my high-security potato chip storage facility and eat some chips!

I feel better already.

CHAPTER 9

THE CHIP THIEF

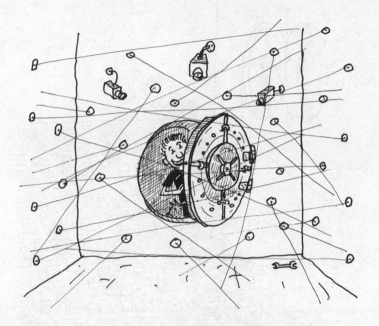

The good thing about a high-security potato chip storage facility is that it keeps your chips safe from chip thieves. The *bad* thing about a high-security potato chip storage facility is that it can be quite hard to get into, even for the rightful owner of the chips.

First you have to tiptoe through 1,000 loaded
mousetraps without getting snapped . . .

And then you have to evade a deadly network of 100 laser beams . . .

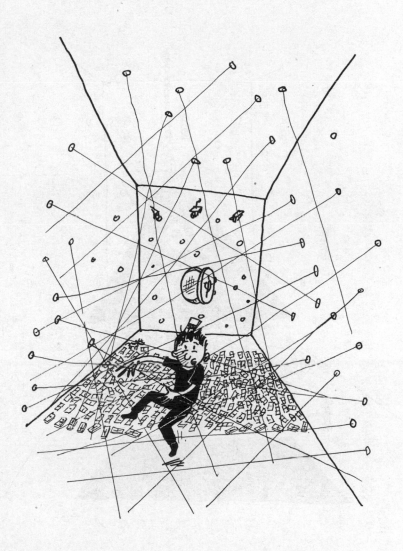

Next you have to avoid getting crushed to death by a ten-ton weight . . .

And then, if you survive all that, you have to . . .

And, in the unlikely event you manage to defeat the very angry duck, then you are faced with the most advanced safe lock ever created—a locking system so complicated, in fact, that there's only one person in the whole world who is smart enough to open it (and that's ME!).

Hold on . . . that's not right!
    The door is unlocked!

Somebody has unlocked my safe!
    Somebody who is *not* me!
    Oh no! My chips!
    My precious chips!
    Somebody has stolen my precious, perfect
potato chips!

Oh, hang on. No they haven't. The bag's still here.
I probably just forgot to lock the door. Oops.

That's funny. There's only one left. I thought I had
more than that.

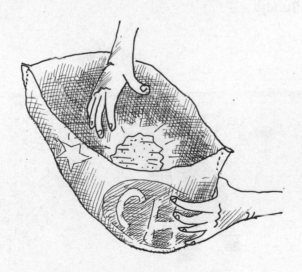

I take the last chip out and bite into it. Mmmm . . .
it tastes as good as ever!

Actually, no it doesn't—it tastes like cardboard!
Ptooey!

That's because it *is* cardboard! Somebody (probably Terry!) snuck in here, unlocked my safe, stole my chips, and replaced them with a single cardboard replica in the hope I wouldn't notice.

I can't believe it. . . . That chip thief Terry has stolen my chips! This means *war*! But first, a rage-filled rant . . . that *rhymes*!

Once Terry was a friend
On whom I could depend.
I could not comprehend
How the fun would ever end.

But now my trust he's trashed.
Into my vault he crashed.
A wicked plan he hatched:
My precious chips he snatched.

He stole my chips, that rotten thief!
It is a crime beyond belief.
My endless grief will not be brief.
For from this pain there's no relief.

I loved those chips and to me it seemed
That all night and day of my chips I dreamed.
Whene'er I thought of my chips I beamed,
But then that chip fiend intervened.

Him and his evil chip-stealing scheme!
How could he be so horribly mean?
It makes me want to shout and scream!
My rage is totally and utterly extreme!

My chips he did so cruelly rob
To shove in his big fat slobbery gob.
It makes me want to sadly sob
To think of my perfectly precious chips
Pinched between his fingertips
And perched upon his drooling lips—
A stolen-chip apocalypse!

From this betrayal I will *never* recover,
We are no longer friends with one another.
I'm warning him now, he'd better take cover,
He's my *worst* ever friend, my *ex*–blood
brother.

Torn photo →

Voodoo Terry

I'm going to hunt that chip thief down!
Him and every last Terry in Terrytown!
They won't be laughing then, those clowns,
I'll turn their smiles into permanent frowns!

I'll wreak my stolen chip revenge!
His punishment will never end!
I'll tell the world of his infamy,
Of how he stole my chips from me.
His name will go down in history
Synonymous with chip thievery!

So now he'd better prepare his tomb—
That gangly-limbed, crazy-eyed,
   curly-haired loon,

'Cause I'm coming at him faster
   than a supersonic boom—
That greedy, grasping, chip-stealing goon.

Closer and closer to him do I zoom—
That traitorous, treacherous
   BFF of a baboon,

And when I get there
It will be safe to assume
That, very soon, you know whom
Will get what's coming
When I deal out his

DOOM!!!

CHAPTER 10

ANDY VERSUS TERRY

I storm out of my high-security potato chip
storage facility and into the kitchen.

Terry and Mel Gibbon are making popcorn
with the lid off the pot. Freshly popped popcorn is
popping in all directions while Mr. Big Shot and
his crew film the whole thing.

"Hey, chip thief!" I yell at Terry. "You stole my chips!"

"No, I didn't," says Terry. "Why would I want to steal your stinky old chips? I'm a movie star now, and I can have all the chips I want!"

"Yeah, well, maybe you stole them before you were a movie star!" I say. "Did you ever think of *that*?"

"No, I didn't think of that," he says, "and I didn't think of anything else, either . . . and I didn't steal your stupid old chips!"

"DID!" I say.

"DIDN'T!" says Terry.

"DID!"

"DIDN'T!"

"DID!"

"DIDN'T!"

"So you deny it?" I say.

"Absolutely!" says Terry, folding his arms.

"Then there's only one way to settle this," I say.

"A fight?" says Mr. Big Shot hopefully.

"No," I say. "A court case. We'll let Judge Gavelhead decide."

"I love it!" says Mr. Big Shot. "Courtroom dramas are box-office gold! Let's go!"

We climb up to the courtroom. Mr. Big Shot
and his crew set up the cameras.

"Lights, camera, action!" he shouts.

Judge Gavelhead bangs his head on the bench.

"Order in the court!" he yells. "Let the case of Andy versus Terry proceed."

"He stole my chips!" I yell, pointing at Terry.

"I object!" says Terry. "He's lying! He's just jealous because I'm a movie star and he's not."

Judge Gavelhead turns to me. "Chip-stealing is a serious crime," he says. "What evidence do you have to support this extraordinary accusation?"

"Well, Your Honor," I say, "I have prepared a detailed diagram showing how the accused didst—on the night in question—with evil chip-stealing aforethought—use a pair of the most technologically advanced mousetrap-proof stilts ever invented to evade the high-security measures of my high-security potato chip storage facility and STEAL MY CHIPS! Behold, Exhibit A!"

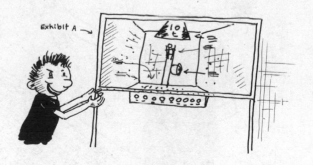

Exhibit A →

EVER INVENTED TO BREAK INTO MY
HIGH-SECURITY POTATO CHIP STORAGE
FACILITY AND STEAL MY POTATO CHIPS.

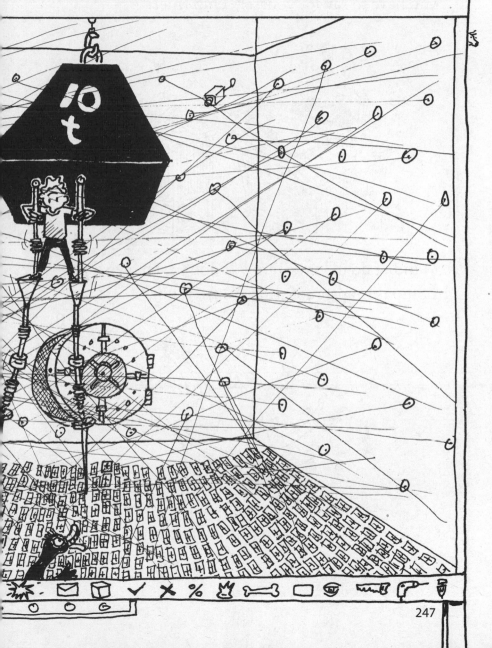

"Well," says Judge Gavelhead. "This looks like an open-and-shut case." He turns to Terry. "What do you have to say for yourself, chip thief?"

"I didn't do it!" says Terry. "I don't even own a pair of mousetrap-proof stilts, Your Honor."

"Not anymore you don't," I say, "because you *ate* them to get rid of the evidence!"

"Did not!" says Terry.

"Did!" I say.

"Order in the court!" says Judge Gavelhead. He bangs his head on the bench.

He turns to me. "Do you wish to call any witnesses?"

"Yes, I most certainly do," I say. "I'd like to call the very angry duck to the stand. She saw the whole thing."

The very angry duck waddles angrily to the witness box.

I step as close to the very angry duck as I dare. "Quack once if the chip thief who stole my chips is in this courtroom," I say.

The very angry duck looks around angrily and quacks.

"Thank you," I say. I point to Terry. "Quack again if I'm now pointing to that chip thief."

The very angry duck quacks.

"Thank you," I say. "No further questions. I rest my case."

"That's not proof!" says Terry. "That duck will quack at anything!"

The very angry duck quacks again.

"See?" says Terry.

Judge Gavelhead bangs his head.

"ORDER IN THE COURT!"

"Quack!"

The judge bangs his head. "Would the chip thief like to call a witness?"

"Yes," says Terry. "I call on Mel Gibbon."

Mel Gibbon swings across the courtroom on a vine and drops down into the witness box.

"Do you know me?" says Terry.

"Yes," says Mel, "you're my *best friend*."

"Thank you," says Terry. "And in all the time that we've been best friends, have you ever known me to steal anybody's chips?"

"No, never," says Mel.

"Thank you," says Terry. "I rest my case."

"Objection!" I say. "Terry and Mel only met each other a few hours ago. And would you take the word of a monkey over that of a duck? Because that's what Mel is—he's a monkey!"

"Objection, Your Honor!" says Mel. "I'm not a monkey, I'm a gibbon!"

"Same thing," I say.

"Is not," says Mel.

"Is so!"

"Is not!"

"Is so!"

Judge Gavelhead bangs his head.

   "ORDER!" he shouts.

   "GIBBON!" yells Mel.

   "MONKEY!" I yell back.

   "QUACK!" says the very angry duck.

"Court dismissed!" says Judge Gavelhead. "I've got a headache."

He stands up and leaves the courtroom.

"Phew!" says Terry. "I'm glad we got that sorted out."

"But we didn't," I say.

"Yes, we did," he says. "It's pretty obvious that *I* didn't do it."

"But you *did* do it!" I say.

"I didn't!"

"DID!"

"DIDN'T!"

"DID!"

"DIDN'T!"

"There's only one way to settle this," I say.

"A fight?" says Mr. Big Shot hopefully.

"Yes," I say, "but not just any ordinary fight—an *epic interstellar space battle!*"

"Perfect!" says Mr. Big Shot. "Epic interstellar space battles are box-office gold! Lights, camera, action!"

"Hang on," I say.

"What's the matter?" says Terry. "You're not chickening out, are you?"

"No, I'm hulking up," I say. "And you'd better do the same unless you want me to squash you like a bug."

"Good idea," says Terry. "Thanks, Andy."

"Don't mention it," I say. "What are ex–best friends for?"

We hulk up as fast as we can.

"Let the epic interstellar space battle begin," I say.

I grab two passing flying saucers and crash them together over Terry's ears.

He pulls the moon from its orbit and kicks it at me . . .

HARD!

I catch a meteor shower in my mouth and spit the meteors back at him.

He grabs me around the neck and pushes my face into the sun. "Hot enough for you, Andy?" he yells.

I break free, grab *him* around the neck, and push *his* face into the sun. "Hope you're wearing lots of sunscreen!" I say.

I don't think he is, though, because his head has caught on fire.

"That's it," he says. "Now you've *really* done it!"

Terry takes the rings from around Saturn and frisbees them at me.

I'm sliced into at least a dozen sections, which, even for a space fight, is going too far, so I have no option but to end it by . . .

shoving him into a super-massive black hole!

"Are you ready to admit you stole my chips now?"
I say. But I get no answer. "Terry?" I say.

Still nothing. "TERRY!" I yell.

But he *still* doesn't reply.

Uh-oh.

I reach into the black hole and pull him out. The extreme gravitation has stretched and pulled his body so much that he looks like he's made of spaghetti.

That's when I hear a familiar sound.

It's Jill! And her space cats!

"Andy?" she says. "What are you doing out here in space? And what happened to Terry—why does he look like a strand of spaghetti?"

"We were having an epic interstellar space battle,"
I say, "and I pushed him into a black hole."

"That's not very nice!" says Jill.

"But he broke into my high-security potato chip
storage facility and stole my chips."

"No, he didn't," says Jill.

"Yes, he did," I say. "He's a dirty, stinking,
rotten, chip-stealing chip thief!"

"No, he's not," says Jill. "Terry did *not* steal your chips."

"How can you be so sure?" I say.

"Because it was *me*," says Jill, "but I didn't *steal* them, I just *borrowed* them."

"But how did you evade the mousetraps, the laser beams, the ten-ton weight, and the very angry duck?" I say.

"With my flying cats, of course!" says Jill.

THE DAY JILL *BROKE* INTO ANDY'S HIGH-SECURITY CHIP STORAGE FACILITY AND *BORROWED* HIS CHIPS.

"And the safe?" I say. "How did you unlock that?"

"It wasn't that hard," says Jill. "It was already open. You're not mad at me, are you?"

"No," I sigh. "I just wish you'd told me."

"I *did*!" she says. "I wrote an IOU on a chip-shaped piece of cardboard and left it in the chip bag."

"I thought that was a chip and I ate it!" I say.

"Oh, good!" says Jill. "Then I won't have to pay you back."

"JILL!" I yell.

"Just joking, Andy," says Jill. "I know how important your chips are to you."

"I think we *all* know how important Andy's chips are to him," says Terry. "Which is why *I* would never try to steal them."

"I guess I owe you an apology, Terry," I say. "I'm sorry I accused you of stealing my chips, took you to court, crashed flying saucers over your head, spat meteors at you, set your head on fire, and pushed you into a black hole."

"Don't worry about it," says Terry. "Let's just forget about all that and be best friends again . . . forever!"

"But what about Mel?" I say. "I thought *he* was your best friend."

"Not in *real* life," says Terry. "That was just acting. I mean, he's a funny guy and I really like him, but you will always be my best friend, Andy—my best *best* friend."

"And you'll always be mine!" I say.

"CUT!" barks Mr. Big Shot through his megaphone as he flies in on his space director's chair. "That's perfect! Brilliant! It's the action-packed, twist-in-the-tale, feel-good ending the movie needed."

"You filmed all that?" I say.

"You bet," says Mr. Big Shot. "I got the whole thing! The public is going to lap it up! You three are going to be BIG movie stars!"

"Me, too?" I say.

"Yes!" says Mr Big Shot. "Every movie needs a supervillain! You'll be the one everybody *loves* to hate!"

"What about me?" says Jill. "And Silky? Will *we* be in it?"

"Of course!" says Mr. Big Shot. "*Intergalactic space-animal rescue service* . . . hilarious!"

"But it's not meant to be funny," says Jill. "Space-animal rescue is a serious business."

But Mr. Big Shot doesn't hear Jill. He's already on his way back to Earth.

"See you on opening night!" he shouts.

CHAPTER 11

BIG-SHOT MOVIE STARS

Hi, my name's Andy. I used to write books, but I'm too busy to do that anymore because now I'm a famous big-shot movie star.

This is my friend Terry. He's a famous big-shot movie star, too.

And this is our friend Jill and her cat Silky. They're famous big-shot movie stars as well.

And so is Jill's donkey, Mr. Hee-Haw.

And her cow, Pat.

In fact, ALL of Jill's animals are FAMOUS BIG-SHOT MOVIE STARS!!!

Well, when I say we are all famous big-shot movie stars, I mean, we're *going* to be . . . just as soon as our movie comes out.

I guess if you're like most movie fans, you're probably wondering exactly *when* the movie is going to come out. Well, as a matter of fact, we're having a star-studded, red-carpet movie premiere at the treehouse tomorrow night . . . AND YOU'RE INVITED!

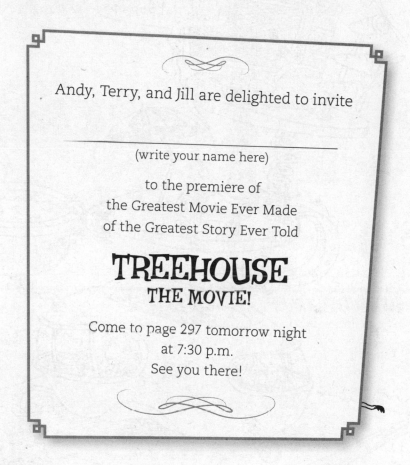

Andy, Terry, and Jill are delighted to invite

_____

(write your name here)

to the premiere of
the Greatest Movie Ever Made
of the Greatest Story Ever Told

TREEHOUSE
THE MOVIE!

Come to page 297 tomorrow night
at 7:30 p.m.
See you there!

Life has changed quite a lot for us since we became movie-stars-in-waiting.

Terry and I now have Hollywood movie star–style pop-up trailers instead of bedrooms.

And we've got custom-built hot-rod limousines
to get around the tree . . . we don't have to walk
anywhere.

We've even got our own Treehouse Walk of Fame.

It's not *all* great, though. For instance, it's kind of hard to see where we're going because we have to wear shades all the time. (When you're a movie star, shades are pretty much compulsory.)

I also kind of miss being able to catch up with Terry and Jill without having to go through agents, managers, personal assistants, and publicists.

PRIVATE
Caught anything yet?
Patience! He'll bite.
Sure, Andy, I'll get my people to talk to your people and we'll set up something.

Plus, we have to spend a lot of time each day trying to avoid the paparazzi.

And, as if the life of movie-stars-in-waiting wasn't already busy enough, we have to prepare the treehouse for the movie premiere tomorrow night.

We're expecting a lot of people—and animals—so we've got to get our open-air movie theater ready.

We'll need at least ten thousand more chairs . . .

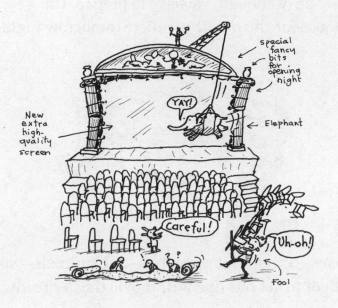

a long roll of red carpet . . .

and we'll have to pop at least ten million pieces of
popcorn.

But don't worry, I'm sure we'll get it all done
in time.

See you tomorrow night!

CHAPTER 12

COWHOUSE: THE MOOO-VIE

Wow—no time at all seems to have passed since the end of the last chapter, and yet it's already tomorrow night right now. Welcome to our movie premiere!

EVERYONE is coming.

In fact, they should be here already, because the movie is due to start in ten minutes and the only ones here are Terry, Jill, me, and you.

But where is everybody else?

"Terry, you *did* send out all the invitations, didn't you?" I say.

"Yes," says Terry. "I gave them all to Bill the Postman to post."

"And all my animals know about it," says Jill. "They've really been looking forward to it!"

"So where are they?" I say.

Jill shrugs. "I don't know," she says.

"Oh, look, here comes someone now!" says Terry, pointing.

We see a group of animals, chattering and chirping, approaching from the edge of the forest.

"Okay," I say, "everybody, just act cool. There's probably going to be a *riot* when they recognize us!"

"Yeah," says Terry. "Lucky we've got these little velvet ropes to protect us."

But instead of heading toward our tree, the animals walk right past our searchlights, our velvet ropes, and our red carpet, and head deeper into the forest.

"That's weird," I say.

"Yes," says Jill. "They were talking about a movie, too, although they weren't saying 'movie'—they were saying '*mooo*-vie.'"

I gasp.

"What?" says Terry.

"It's those spy cows I was trying to tell you about," I say. "I think they've stolen our movie—and our opening night as well!"

"I already *told* you, Andy," says Jill. "I just don't think cows would do that. They're not interested in movies—unless the movies are about grass, of course."

ABOVE: *An artist's impression of a poster for the sort of movie Jill thinks cows would be interested in.*

"Perhaps you're right, Jill," I say. "Maybe *ordinary* cows are not interested in most movies—but these are no ordinary cows. These are *mooo-vie-making* spy cows. You believe me, don't you, Terry?"

"No, I don't," says Terry, "and I believe in a lot of pretty unbelievable stuff."

"Okay, fine," I say, "let's just follow those animals, and maybe you'll believe it when you see it."

We set off into the forest.

We can hear the sound of an excited crowd in the distance. More and more animals and people appear in front of us, around us, and behind us.

We come over a rise and see a vast open area packed with people, animals, and cows . . . *especially* cows . . . all sitting in front of a super-giant mooo-vie screen.

"Look at that," I say, "*Cowhouse: The Mooo-vie!*
Now do you believe me?"

"Shh!" says Terry. "The mooo-vie's about to start."

"Hey," says Terry. "Those cows look just like us."

"Yeah," I say. "Except they're *cows*!"

"Shh!" says Jill.

"Hey," says Terry, "that's just like when *my* pants were on fire."

"I *know*," I say. "That's where they got the idea!"

"Shh," says Jill.

"Hey," says Jill, "that's just like what happened to Silky."

"No, it's not," says Terry. "She turned into a *catnary*, not an udderfly."

"Shh!" I say.

"Hey," says Terry, "that's just like my Ninja Snails."

"I know," I say. "Those cows have stolen *all* our stories."

"Shh!" says Jill.

"Hey," says Terry, "that's just like when the shark ate *my* underpants."

"Duh!" I say, jumping up in front of him. "Don't you get it yet?"

"Sit down, Andy," says Jill. "I can't see the mooo-vie."

"Cows are funny," says Terry.

"They're also thieves," I say. "They stole that idea from *Barky the Barking Dog*."

"Shh," says Jill. "I can't hear what Mooey is saying."

"Remember when we had an epic interstellar space battle, Andy?" says Terry.

"I sure do," I say. "And it looks like the cows do, too. They are such copycats."

"I think you mean copy*cows*," says Jill.

"Oh, that's so sweet," says Jill.

"But it's OUR story," I say.

"No, it's not," says Terry. "We're best friends, not barn buddies."

"Hey!" says Terry. "That's exactly how *our* story ends . . .

"Wait a minute . . .

"*WAIT* a minute . . .

"Hang on . . .

"Just one more minute . . .

"THOSE THIEVING COWS STOLE OUR MOVIE!" yells Terry. "THEY COPIED ALL OUR IDEAS!"

"That's what I've been trying to tell you all along!" I say.

"Yeah," says Terry. "I know. Sorry I didn't listen to you. But look on the bright side: everybody seems to have liked the cows' movie, so they're *sure* to like ours, too."

"Well, they would have," I say, "but if we release our movie now, everybody will say we copied our ideas from a bunch of cows!"

"I think that should be a *herd* of cows," says Jill.

"That's not important now!" I say.

"Just because you're upset," Jill says, "that's no reason not to use the correct term for a group of cows."

"But we *didn't* copy them," says Terry. "They copied us!"

"I know that, and you know that, and Jill knows that," I say, "but nobody else knows that. We'll just have to make another movie about how the cows stole our first movie . . . but this time we'll make sure the cows don't know anything about the movie we're making."

"Um, Andy," says Jill, "I think—"

"Not now, Jill," I say, "I have to talk to Mr. Big Shot."

"But it's important."

"It will have to wait!" I say. "We need to get started on our next movie right away. Let's find Mr. Big Shot and get filming."

"Here he comes now," says Terry.

"Hey, Mr. Big Shot," I say. "We need to talk to you!"

"Hi, gang!" he says. "Great movie, huh?"

"Well, kind of," I say, "but it was *our* movie!"

"Yeah," says Mr. Big Shot, shrugging. "What can I say? The cows got there first. Your movie is ruined. But, hey, that's show business."

"But we've got a great idea for *another* movie," I say, "and we'd like you to direct it. We want to get started right now before the cows steal this idea as well."

"I'm sorry," says Mr. Big Shot, "but the cows have already hired me to direct their next movie. It's about some cows who steal a movie idea about a movie about idea-stealing cows. It's going to be even bigger, better, and *creamier* than *Cowhouse: The Mooo-vie*. In fact, we're off to Hollywood right now! These cows are going to be BIG stars!"

"Déjà vu," whispers Terry.

"*Déjà moo*, you mean," I say.

CHAPTER 13

THE LAST CHAPTER

We get back to the treehouse and sit on the couch.

"So what do we do now?" I say.

"I don't know," says Terry. "What did we used to do before we were about to be movie stars?"

"Beats me," I say.

"You used to make books together," says Jill. "You wrote the words, Andy, and, Terry, you drew the pictures."

The videophone rings.

"Uh-oh," I say. "That will be Mr. Big Nose. He's probably heard about the movie. He's not going to be happy."

"You answer it, Andy," says Terry.

"I'm not answering it," I say. "I'm scared."

"Me too," says Terry. "Let's hide behind the couch."

Jill sighs. "I'll do it," she says.

Jill answers the videophone, and Mr. Big Nose's face fills the screen. He looks bigger and crosser than ever.

"WHERE ARE ANDY AND TERRY?" he yells.

"They're hiding behind the couch," says Jill.

"I'm not surprised," yells Mr. Big Nose. "I heard those clowns ruined the movie!"

"It wasn't *their* fault," says Jill. "It was the cows. They copied all the ideas and made their *own* movie."

"COWS?!" yells Mr. Big Nose.

I jump up. "Yes," I say. "Cows! But these were no ordinary cows. They were *spy* cows! I tried to warn everybody, but no one would listen to me, not even Terry."

Terry jumps up from behind the couch. "That's not fair, Andy," he says. "You were covered in prickles and had a cowpat on your head. You can't blame us for thinking it was just another one of your crazy schemes to wreck the movie, like the scribbling, the flying plates, and the Andy invasion."

"What?" yells Mr. Big Nose. "You tried to *wreck* the movie?!"

"No," I say. "I tried to *save* the movie. The plates and the scribbletorium explosion were both accidents. And I *tried* to stop the Andys, but *they* wouldn't listen to me, *either*. And, by the way, I also practically saved the entire planet from being empuddled by a giant puddle!"

"THAT'S ENOUGH!" says Mr. Big Nose. "This whole explanation is the most ridiculous thing I've ever heard. In fact, it's so ridiculous, it sounds like the plot of one of your books. Speaking of which, if I can't have a movie, then I'll have a book instead. By midnight tonight. Without fail. Or else! GOOD-BYE!"

"Well," says Terry, "that all seemed to work out quite nicely."

"Yeah," I say, "except that we've got to write a book by midnight."

"No problem!" says Terry. "Midnight it is.

"Hang on . . .

"Wait a minute . . .

"Wait *another* minute . . .

"Hang on . . .

"Just one more minute . . .
Do you mean midnight . . . *tonight?*"

"Yes," says Jill. "Midnight *tonight*."

"*Big* problem!" says Terry. "That's hardly any time at all, and we don't even have an idea for a book because we've been so busy with the movie!"

"That's *it*!" I say. "We'll write the book about making the movie! Mr. Big Nose said it was a ridiculous story, so it's perfect!"

"You mean we're going to write a book about writing a book about making a movie about writing a book?" says Terry. "That sounds complicated."

"That's because it *is*!" I say. "We'd better get started before it gets any more complicated."

"But what about the cows?" says Terry. "Won't they just steal all our ideas and bring out the book before us?"

"No, of course not," I say. "Cows can't write books."

"Good point," says Terry.

WHY COWS CAN'T WRITE BOOKS.
Stupid Cow hooves!!
They don't have hands.
I'm winning!
I'm coming second!
They get distracted by their favorite sport—udder racing.
They'd rather be out dancing.
They are too busy planning a moon landing.
x+y=56

"Okay," says Terry. "We'll call it *The Book of the Book of the Movie of the Book*."

"I'm not sure about that," I say. "How about *The 78-Story Treehouse*? It will be easier for our readers to remember."

"Good thinking, Andy," says Terry. "Let's get to work."

"but then a bolt of lightning shot out of the electricorn's horn,

"and set them on fire."

I remember that!

"hit the back of my pants,

ZAP!

"He's with a film crew. They're making a Treehouse movie."

"Wow!" says Jill. "How come you're not there?"

I sigh. "The big-shot Hollywood director Mr. Big Shot said he didn't need a narrator."

"Isn't it called a 'voice-over' when it's in a movie?"

"Yeah, well, whatever it's called, Mr. Big Shot didn't want it."

"That's too bad," says Jill. "Still, a movie—that's pretty exciting!"

"I guess so," I say, "If you like electricorns, that is."

"*Electricorns?*" says Jill.

"Yeah," I say. "Terry used the combining machine to combine an electric eel and a unicorn. They're filming a reenactment."

"This I've *got* to see!" says Jill. "Good luck hatching the giant unhatched egg, Andy."

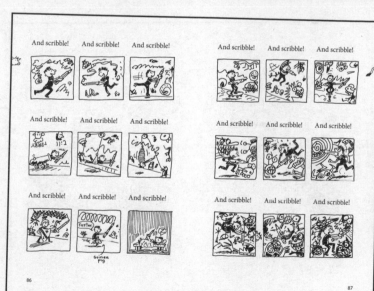

And to make things worse, the puddle is getting bigger.

And bigger.

And bigger.

100

101

"Hey!" yells Mr. Big Shot. "No Andys on the set!"

Mel Gibbon is whacking golf balls at the Andys, trying to hold them back, but there are too many Andys . . . and not enough golf balls.

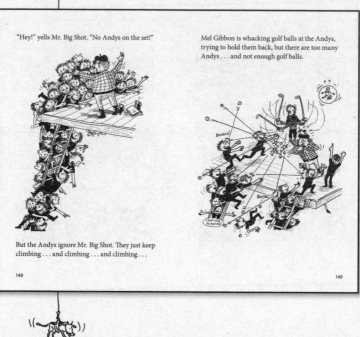

But the Andys ignore Mr. Big Shot. They just keep climbing . . . and climbing . . . and climbing . . .

148

149

First you have to tiptoe through 1,000 loaded mousetraps without getting snapped . . .

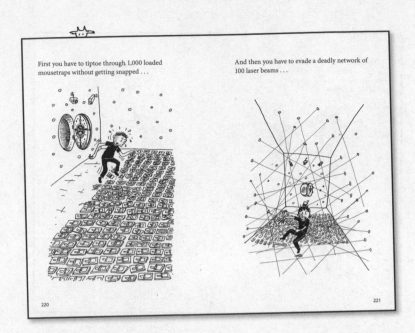

220

And then you have to evade a deadly network of 100 laser beams . . .

221

We climb up to the courtroom. Mr. Big Shot and his crew set up the cameras.
"Lights, camera, action!" he shouts.

242

243

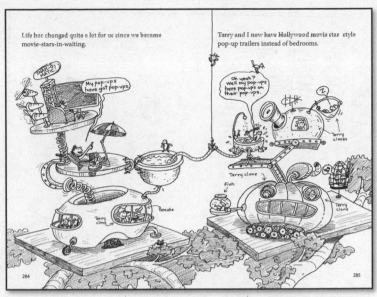

Life has changed quite a lot for us since we became movie-stars-in-waiting.

My pop-ups have got pop-ups

SMAK-O-MATIC?

Terry clone

Pancake

Terry and I now have Hollywood movie star style pop-up trailers instead of bedrooms.

Oh yeah? Well my pop-ups have pop-ups on their pop-ups.

Terry clones

Terry clone

fish

Terry clone

284

285

"Shh!" says Terry. "The mooo-vie's about to start."

COWHOUSE: THE MOOO-VIE

STARRING:
BLUEBELL
DAISY
AND
BUTTERCUP

Nup! Never! No!

"Hey," says Terry. "Those cows look just like us."
"Yeah," I say. "Except they're *cows!*"
"Shh!" says Jill.

308

309

"It's action-packed!" says Terry. "Our best yet! Just one question."

"What is it?" I say.

"How are we going to get it to Mr. Big Nose on time?"

"I'm not sure," I say, "but we need to think of something fast because it's five minutes to midnight!"

"Look!" says Jill. "The giant unhatched egg is cracking—it must be about to hatch!"

"I wonder what it will be," says Terry. "I hope it's not a cow."

"Don't worry," says Jill. "Cows don't hatch from eggs."

"But birds do," I say. "Maybe it will be a really fast one, like a supersonic sparrow or a fuel-injected falcon, and it could deliver our book for us."

"It's a *tortoise*!" says Jill.

"Oh, great!" I say. "Just what we *don't* need. One of the slowest animals in the world. A tortoise isn't going to be any help to us at all."

354

"I wouldn't be so sure about that," says Jill. "See the engine and the exhaust pipes coming out of its shell? If I'm not mistaken, it's a *turbo tortoise*, one of the *fastest* animals in the world."

THE FASTEST (AND SLOWEST)

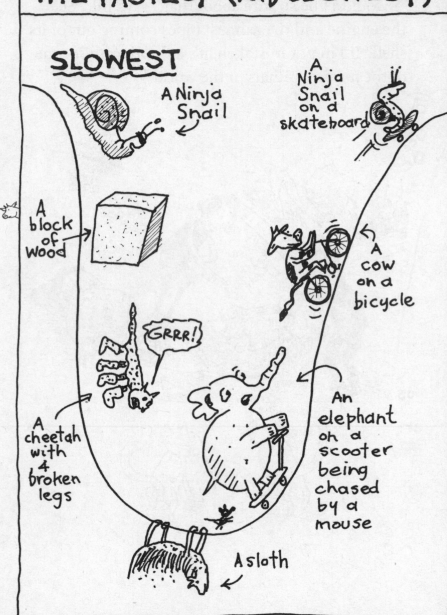

SLOWEST

A Ninja Snail

A Ninja Snail on a skateboard

A block of wood

A cow on a bicycle

GRRR!

A cheetah with 4 broken legs

An elephant on a scooter being chased by a mouse

A sloth

ANIMALS IN THE WORLD CHART

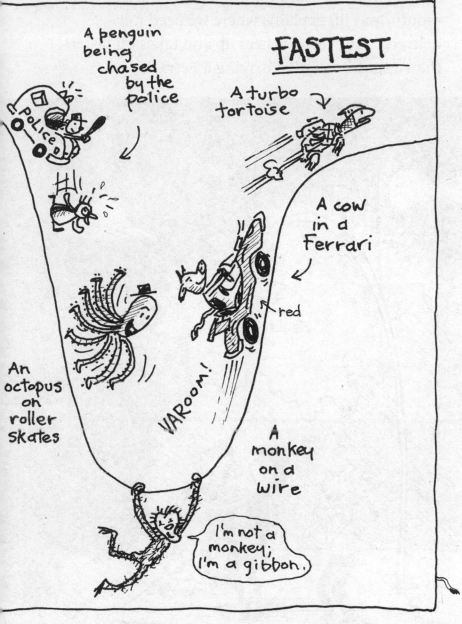

We put the manuscript in the turbo tortoise's mouth, and Jill explains where we need it delivered. The tortoise fires up and takes off faster than a speeding bullet driving a Ferrari.

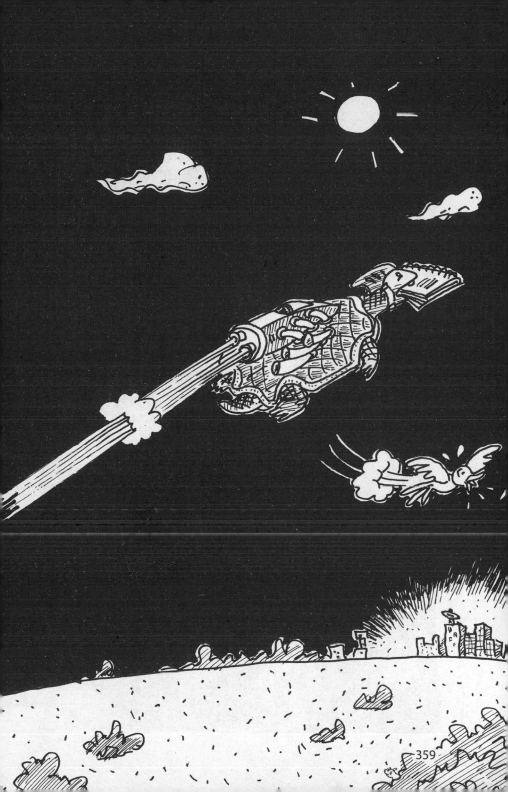

"Mission accomplished!" says Terry, peering through our night telescope as the turbo tortoise crashes through Mr. Big Nose's office window. "It's 11:59 p.m. and 59 seconds. The turbo tortoise has delivered the book with one second to spare!"

"Yay!" I say, grabbing Terry's hand and Jill's hand and raising them in triumph.

MEOW SQUAWK MOO!
COCK-A-DOODLE-DOO!
HONK OINK NEIGH!
SQUEAK ROAR BRAY!

"Uh-oh," says Jill, looking at her intergalactic space-animal rescue service emergency pager. "A gorilla has crash-landed a banana rocket on Planet Kong. See you both later. I'm sorry the cows stole your movie, but your book is great! Much better than a silly old *mooo*-vie any day!"

"Well, that was a fun day," says Terry. "What are we going to do tomorrow?"

"I'll tell you what you're going to do," says a voice behind us.

We turn to see a mysterious woman wearing a
brightly colored headscarf, large gold earrings, and
a necklace made of gold coins. She's holding
a crystal ball in her hand.

"Who are you?" I say.

"I am Madame Know-It-All," she says. "I know all and see all, and I already know that you are going to build me a level where I can set up my fortune-telling tent and end my wandering ways."

"What a good idea!" says Terry. "It will be great to have a full-time fortune teller—then we'll always know what's going to happen next! And we can build some other new levels while we're at it."

"I knew you were going to do that as well," says Madame Know-It-All.

"Wow!" I say.

"I knew you were going to say that, too," she says.

"What's going to happen next?" says Terry.

"Nothing," she says, "because it's the end of the book."

"I knew that," I say.

"I knew it first," says Madame Know-It-All.

THE 78-STORY TREEHOUSE

BONUS MATERIALS

Dear Andy Griffiths,

Thank you for finishing these sentences.

xo,

◨ SQUARE
FISH

The number 78 is . . . an easier and much quicker way of saying 6 x 13 or 5 x 15.6 or 4 x 19.5 or 3 x 26 or 2 x 39.

My favorite movie . . . is a toss-up between *King Kong* and *2001: A Space Odyssey*. Weirdly they both feature monkeys, and if you've read *The 78-Story Treehouse*, you'll know how much I HATE monkeys.

Seven is . . . the number of secretive children who used to solve crimes in one of my favorite book series growing up called The Secret Seven by Enid Blyton.

Eight is . . . the number that if you put it on its side represents infinity . . . and that's a really big super-never-ever-ending number!

If there's one thing I know . . . it's that you should never push your best friend's head into the sun because he will probably do it to back to you, and if you don't have sunscreen on your head, it will definitely catch on fire.

You should never . . . try to steal my chips because I keep them in a high-security potato chip storage facility protected by 1000 loaded mousetraps, 100 laser beams, a 10-ton weight, and 1 very angry duck.

If 18 monkeys pounded on a typewriter . . . for one hour, they would probably come up with a book called JS!!PEFUkw092&7encbqpe9fnsou7n; jfn%weiofbKSO*IUBRn9un90n9$%&(E67852u, but I'm not sure anybody would want—or even be able—to read it.

The best spies . . . are spy cows. Nobody ever suspects them because everybody just thinks they're cows . . . and they are, but they are also spies, and they are always trying to steal your movie ideas.

How come you forgot to ask about . . . that time I fought a giant puddle all by myself because my stupid, dumb dum-dum of a friend and fellow puddlefighter Terry couldn't help me because he was busy being a big shot Hollywood movie star? It was the most epic puddlefight in history . . . I wish they'd filmed that.

Dear Terry Denton,

Thank you for finishing these sentences.

xo,

SQUARE FISH

The number 18 is . . . the number of bones in Andy's head.

My favorite movie . . . is *Eraserhead*, which is a movie all about erasers! They are bad, mean erasers. Instead of erasing the drawings, they erase the illustrator . . . slowly, bit by bit, until he's all gone.

Seven is . . . how many legs Otto, my pet octopus, has. Why? Well, that is a very sad story for another day!!

Eight is . . . how many legs Otto would prefer to have. He wants me to buy him a new robotic leg, but where can you buy robotic octopus legs? And can they be trusted?

If there's one thing I know . . . drawing Treehouse books is very hard work because there are about one thousand drawings in each book. But working up the treehouse with Andy and the penguins is buckets of FUN!!!

You should never . . . sleepwalk in a treehouse, or you may fall into the shark tank and sharks are always very hungry at night.

If 78 monkeys pounded on a typewriter . . . eventually they would write an Andy Griffiths book.

The best spies . . . would never leave home without a seven-legged octopus. (Well, that's what Otto says.)

How come you forgot to ask about . . . Nine-legged octopuses!!!!

Andy and Terry get stuck babysitting Mr. Big Nose's three grandchildren for the day. Good thing there's so many fun things to do in their 91-story treehouse! After all, how much trouble can they manage to get into in just *one* day?

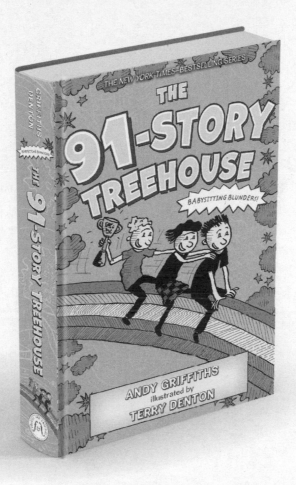

Keep reading for an excerpt!

CHAPTER 1

THE 91-STORY TREEHOUSE

Hi, my name is Andy.

This is my friend Terry.

We live in a tree.

Well, when I say "tree," I mean treehouse.
And when I say "treehouse," I don't just mean
any old treehouse—I mean a 91-*story* treehouse!
(It used to be a 78-story treehouse, but we've
added another 13 stories.)

So what are you waiting for?
Come on up!

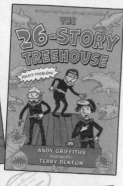
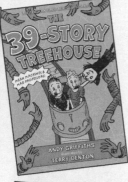